Phoebe Flower's Adventures:

Phoebe's *Best* Best Friend

by **Barbara Roberts**

illustrated by Kate Sternberg

ADVANTAGE BOOKS

Published by Advantage Books
1001 Spring Street, Suite 206
Silver Spring, MD 20910

Library of Congress Cataloging-in-Publication Data
Roberts, Barbara A., 1947-
    Phoebe's best best friend / by Barbara A. Roberts ;
illustrated by Kate Sternberg.
        p. cm. — (Phoebe Flower's adventures ; 3)
        Summary: Third-grader Phoebe is so happy to have a "best friend,"
but at the same time she is having more trouble concentrating on her
school work.

    ISBN   0-9660366-9-7
    [1. Best Friends—Fiction. 2. Friendship—Fiction. 3. Schools—Fiction.]
    4. Attention-deficit hyperactivity disorder—Fiction.]
    I. Sternberg, Kate, 1954- ill. II. Title

    PZ7.R5395 Ph 2000
    [Fic]—dc21   00-053590

                10 9 8 7 6 5 4 3 2 1
                Printed in the U.S.A.

Contents

This book is dedicated to Pam Heneghan, my friend of 48 years.
Pam...
    ... shares with me the gift of rich childhood memories.
    ... provides the ultimate example of strength and courage.
    ... blesses me with a lifelong friendship.

I also want to thank Kathleen K. Walker. Kathleen's wit, warmth and passionate love of life, inspired the character Mrs. Walkerspeaking and day after day, Kathleen continues to exhilarate those who know and love her.

Thanks,
Barb Roberts

To "Bahb"
♥
K. S.

1
Introducing
...the One, the Only
...Gloria

There are three fabulous things about third grade. First of all, it's not second grade, so that means I am closer to being out of school forever. Second of all, I have Mr. Blister, the only man teacher in the school. Everybody wanted him for a teacher! Third of all, and most fabulous of all, I have a best friend! I have never had a best friend before. I don't think I can count Robbie. He's like my brother. He only acts like my friend when we play alone. If his friends ask him to play football, he won't let me go with him even though he knows I can zigzag run faster than any of the boys. He doesn't like to do girl stuff, either, like talk on the phone when he's doing his homework. And, when I sit next to him on the bus and I want to tell him a secret, he won't let me lean close to him and whisper it in his ear. I say, "Robbie, if you want to hear this, you better let me sit close and whisper it in your ear."

Robbie always says, "Shh, Phoebe! Get away from me."

My best friend's name is Gloria Von Kloppenstein. She sang the solo in the first grade concert. She also sang the solo in the second grade concert and I, Phoebe Flower, played the piano while she sang. The audience clapped and cheered for both of us.

Miss Prissy Fasola, the music teacher at my school, told me that, if I wanted to learn to play the piano for the second grade concert, I would have to practice, practice, practice. She said I could stay after school and she would help me. Miss Fasola said that sometimes Gloria Von Kloppenstein could stay too, and we would practice together.

When I first thought about practicing with Gloria, I thought, "YUCK!" I never liked her. I wanted to be the one to sing the solo. So, the first day we stayed after school to practice together, I said (just to make Gloria mad), "This will be so much fun won't it, Gloria Von Clappenstein?" Gloria laughed so hard and so long I thought she would choke. After that, we became best friends. Gloria said, "Phoebe, you are the funniest person I have ever known."

Gloria isn't funny at all, but, boy, can she laugh! Whenever Gloria is sad I always say, "Gloria, what's the difference between an orange and a matta baby?" "What's a matta baby?" Gloria asks. "Nothing, baby, what's a matta with you?" I answer her.

Gloria laughs and laughs even though she has heard that joke a thousand times.

Gloria gets straight A's in school and she always sits up straight and raises her hand when she wants to talk. She's pretty and smart and she wears the coolest clothes. She is very quiet and never gets yelled at for talking too much or for getting out of her seat to get a drink of water when she's not supposed to. Gloria doesn't have untied shoelaces that look like dirty spaghetti, either.

Gloria lives with her father and her older brother. Her mother died when she was two years old. I asked her once if she missed her mother and Gloria said, "Yeah, I miss her, I guess. I only remember a little bit about her, but my dad is really nice. He makes the best chocolate chip cookies in the whole wide world. He sometimes reads me two books a day and he takes me to the movies every single month. Maybe you could go with us sometime, Phoebe. "I would love to, Gloria! I've never been to the movies with a friend before," I told her.

One night, when we were sitting at the dinner table, I asked my mom if I could invite Gloria over to play.

"Gloria, the girl who sang the solo in the first grade concert?" Amanda asked.

"Yes, that's the Gloria I mean; the one, the only, Gloria Von Kloppenstein! She's my best friend," I said.

"You must be kidding! Why would Gloria want to be your best friend? She could be anybody's best friend. Give me one good reason, Phoebe. Is this some kind of a joke,

Mom?" Amanda asked in a mean voice.

"Of course you can invite Gloria over, Phoebe," Mom answered, "and, Amanda, it is no joke. I can think of one million reasons why Gloria would want to be Phoebe's friend. First of all, and best of all, Phoebe is kind. Now, could you try to be kinder to your sister, please?"

"I guess I can try," Amanda answered.

"How about tomorrow?" I asked my mom. "Gloria can ride home from school with me on the bus. We can play in my tree house and jump rope and she can stay for dinner and we can watch TV. Then Gloria can stay overnight. We'll tell ghost stories and we can ride the bus back to school in the morning. How's that for a great idea?"

"Be careful, Mom," Amanda warned, "next thing you know, Phoebe will want us to buy a bigger house so that Gloria can move in."

"Slow down, Phoebe," Mom said. "Gloria can come tomorrow because I don't have to work, but just to play and stay for dinner. You'll have to do your homework before you play, too."

"Thank you, oh wonderful mother of mine!" I yelled.

"Call her and see if her father says it's okay," Mom told me, "and, while you're at it, call your own father, too. You haven't called him in a week."

"I called Dad yesterday, Mom, and he said he loved hearing from me," Amanda bragged.

"Oh, sure, Mom, I'll call Dad. I know Gloria's father will say 'okay,' though. He's the greatest dad. He makes the best chocolate chip cookies in the whole world," I told Mom.

Gloria's father said she could come home on the bus with me and that he would pick her up at 7:00, after dinner. I couldn't sleep all night. This was going to be the best time ever. I started thinking about what we'd do. We were going to have so much fun.

The next day in school seemed like the longest day of my life. When the bell finally rang for us to get on the bus to go home, I grabbed Gloria's hand and led her to my bus and pushed all the way to the back to find a seat. "Hi, Robbie, this is Gloria Von Kloppenstein. She's my best friend and she is coming over to my house today to play and eat dinner."

"I know Gloria, Phoebe. She's in my class

too. Remember?" Robbie said and turned to look out the bus window.

"I think Robbie's jealous of you," I whispered in Gloria's ear.

Gloria moved to sit closer to me.

2
Rolling
Meatballs

When we got to my house, I pulled Gloria up the sidewalk to the front door. Buddy Dog came bounding out from behind the bushes and started to sniff and lick Gloria. "Do you like dogs, Gloria?" I asked her. "Buddy Dog won't hurt you. He just likes to sniff and lick."

"I don't have a dog, but I'd love to have one," Gloria answered as she reached down and petted Buddy Dog on the head.

"Come on inside and meet Walter and Pam," I said. "Amanda is at cheerleading practice, lucky for us. She thinks she is the boss of the universe. She's my big sister and she's a real pain, if you know what I mean."

Walter was sitting in his high chair eating Cheerios. "Hi, Walter, this is Gloria. Can you say Gloria?" I asked Walter.

"Oreo!" Walter said.

Gloria laughed out loud.

"Hi, Pam," I said to my mother. "I would like you to meet Gloria Von Kloppenstein, my best friend."

My mother turned around from the sink and glared at me with one eyebrow pushed up to her forehead. "Hi, Gloria, I'm Mrs. Flower. It's very nice to meet you. Oh, and by the way, Phoebe, just in case you forgot, I'm 'Mom' to you."

"Oh, I didn't forget, Pam, oops, sorry, I mean, Mom. I just wanted Gloria to know your real name. Maybe she'll want to write you a letter some day." I smiled and Gloria giggled.

"Why don't you girls go out and play and I'll call you when dinner's ready. You can do your homework after dinner. How's that for a good idea, Phoebe?" Mom said.

"Great idea, Mom, but first we have to go upstairs and put on play clothes. I don't want to get my outfit all grass-stained. You know how careful I am."

"No, I don't know how careful you are, but that's a very good idea," Mom answered.

I grabbed Gloria's hand and dragged her up the stairs toward my bedroom.

"Come on, Gloria, we have to hurry," I whispered to her. "We have to sneak into Amanda's room while she's at cheerleading practice. She'll kill me if she knows I'm in her room. She has the neatest stuff."

I pushed open Amanda's door and pointed to the sign that says "KEEP OUT!". Before Gloria knew what I was doing, I pulled open Amanda's closet doors and wiggled inside her closet, past her shoes to the way back corner. "Ah, I found it," I thought to myself. I crawled backwards out of her closet and placed the box I found on Amanda's bed.

"What's in there?" Gloria asked.

"Just wait and see," I told Gloria.

"Wow!" Gloria gasped when I opened the box. "This is so cool. She's got a diary in here. I always wanted one of those. She's even got lipstick and blush and eye shadow."

"What color lipstick is it, Gloria?" I asked. "I wonder if it will go with my tee shirt."

"It's called 'Bubble Gum'," Gloria answered. "Won't Amanda be mad if you put on her lipstick?"

"Sure, she'll be mad, if she finds out," I said as I put on the lipstick. "Amanda is mad all the time, anyway, but she won't find out. Amanda never really notices me. She only thinks about herself."

"Phoebe, I can hear your mother talking to someone and I didn't hear the phone ring. Do you think Amanda's home from practice?" Gloria seemed nervous.

"Yikes, that does sound like her voice! We better get out of here. Hand me the diary and lipstick, Gloria. I don't want you killed the first time you come to visit me." I grabbed the box and threw it in the back of the closet. I took Gloria's hand and we ran down the hall to my room and closed the door behind us.

"Whew! That was a close one!" I said, huffing and puffing.

Mom made spaghetti and meatballs for dinner and Gloria said it was her favorite thing

to eat in the whole world. Amanda told us she was sure she would be picked to be captain of the cheerleading team because her coach told her that she jumped higher than a kangaroo.

"I would love to cheerlead when I get older," Gloria said.

"Maybe I can teach you some cheers after dinner, Gloria," Amanda offered.

"That's okay, Amanda," I said, "Gloria and I have to go to the tree house after dinner and spy on Robbie and his friends. Maybe next time."

"But I really would love to learn some cheers, Amanda. Maybe we'll have time for one," Gloria smiled.

"Phoebe, you look flushed and your lips look very red today. Are you feeling all right?" my mother asked.

"Never felt better, Mom," I answered.

"Yes, your lips look pinkish. Mom's right. Do you have lipstick on, Phoebe?" Amanda stared at me.

"Now where in the world would I get lipstick, Amanda? You're so silly. It must be the spaghetti sauce." I quickly grabbed my fork and picked up a big meatball covered with sauce and shoved into my mouth. I did this so fast that I hit another meatball on my plate. It rolled off the table and splattered onto the floor.

"Oh that was just great, Phoebe!" Amanda said, "Now clean it up."

"Ball, ball," Walter giggled.

"I'll clean it up," my mother said. "Please try to be more careful, Phoebe."

Gloria took one look at me and started laughing so hard she made snorting noises through her nose. She asked to be excused. When she returned she apologized for laughing so hard.

"It wasn't your fault, Gloria, Phoebe is just clumsy," Amanda said." So, the next time you come over, maybe I'll teach you to cheer and you and I can sing some songs together. I sang a solo once in third grade."

"It was only two words, Amanda. I wouldn't really call that a solo. Plus, the next time Gloria comes over we are going to jump rope and use my new jewelry-making kit, right, Gloria?" I asked.

"Sure, Phoebe, but I'll have time to sing, too." Gloria smiled at Amanda.

"Eat your salad, Phoebe," my mom said. "You haven't touched it."

I shoved some salad into my mouth, wishing

Amanda would disappear. A piece of lettuce fell off my plate to the floor. I was sure no one saw it fall. I quickly ducked my head under the table to find the piece of lettuce. Then carefully, I grabbed it between two toes on my right foot and gently lifted it. I thought this was pretty clever, so I lifted it with my toes up to the table and placed the lettuce back on my salad plate.

Gloria started to giggle. Amanda shook her head. Walter stared at my salad plate.

"Phoebe Flower, what are you doing?" My mother was red in the face. "Come into the living room. I have to speak to you now."

"But, Mom," I started.

My mother walked into the living room, turned around to face me. She took her right pointer finger, pointed it to the ground and drew an invisible line. "Do you see this?" she asked.

"What?" I answered.

"The line I just drew with my finger," she answered.

"Yes," I said, but I didn't really see it since it was invisible.

"Well, you have crossed that line, Phoebe Flower. I am angry and you will never ever have another friend over to this house if you don't stop showing off. Do you understand what I am saying?"

"Yes," I gulped.

"Now go in there and finish eating and remember your manners. Use your fork, not your toes!"

3
All Work and Still No Play

Today when I get to school there's a note on my desk that says:

Dear Phoebe,
I had the best time of my whole life at your house yesterday.
Thanks so much for inviting me.
                    Love,
                    Your best friend,
                    Gloria

I don't think I've ever been as happy in my whole life. I want to do cartwheels all around the room. Instead, I look over at Gloria and smile so wide I think the corners of my lips are touching my ears.

"Good morning, boys and girls," says Mr. Blister. "I have a surprise for you today. I'll see if you can guess what it is after I take attendance."

"Robbie," calls Mr. Blister.

"Here!" replies Robbie.

"Isaiah!"

"Here, too!" says Isaiah.

"Elizabeth!"

"Present, Mr. Blister," answers Elizabeth.

"Phoebe!" calls Mr. Blister, ignoring Elizabeth's movie star voice.

"Here!" I reply, smiling at Gloria. I'm so glad we have the same teacher.

Mr. Blister reads on down his list. "Jooling!"

Every head in the classroom turns toward the window side of the room where Mr. Blister is looking. Jooling has hair the color of that delicious black licorice from Fagan's drugstore. It's long and thick and covers part of her eye. Jooling doesn't even look like she heard Mr. Blister call her name.

18

Getting no reply, Mr. Blister gently asks, "Jooling, are you here? Say 'here,' dear!"

Some of the kids in the class start to giggle.

"Jooling is from Korea, boys and girls, and she is the surprise," Mr. Blister explains. "She doesn't speak very much English, but Jooling is very smart. Her mom and dad are studying to become doctors in the United States. Please show her what good friends you can be."

Mr. Blister continues to take attendance.

The rest of the morning, Jooling sits and stares at her desk. I know this because I usually stare out the window and watch the UPS truck deliver packages to the school. At lunch time I remember what Mr. Blister said about being a good friend.

"Gloria, let's ask Jooling to sit with us at lunch," I say.

"Come on, Phoebe," Gloria answers. "Don't you just want it to be you and me."

"Yeah, but she looks so lonely. Let's just ask her," I say.

"Oh, okay!" Gloria agrees.

We both walk over to Jooling's desk. "Hey, Jooling, wanna eat lunch with us?" Gloria asks.

Jooling doesn't even blink her eyes.

"Come on, WE WILL SH—OW YOU THE CAF-E-TER-I-A," I say and stretch out each syllable.

Jooling doesn't move.

"Leave her alone," Gloria says. "She doesn't want to come with us."

Gloria takes my hand and we walk to the cafeteria together.

I love being Gloria's best friend, but it makes schoolwork and homework harder to do. I'm always trying to think of fun things that Gloria and I can do together so that Gloria will keep liking me. Mr. Blister gives us lots of homework, too. Tonight we have to do two pages of math, study twenty-five spelling words and think about the essay we have to write entitled, "What I Am Most Thankful For." Mr. Blister calls on me a lot, too. He says, "Phoebe, you are as flighty as a bumble bee. Try to focus on what we're doing in the classroom." I like him, but he's really not as great as I thought.

Today on the way home from school, I ask Robbie what he's most thankful for. "No way, Phoebe, I'm not telling you that. I don't want you copying my idea and using it for the essay," Robbie says.

"Not this time, Robbie. I know what I'm most thankful for already," I say with a smile, thinking about how I can ask my mom if Gloria can come over on Saturday.

When I walk in the house, Mom is standing at the sink doing the dishes and Walter is sitting in his high chair rubbing crackers in his hair. "Hi, Phoebe, how was your day?" Mom asks with a sigh.

"Just great, Mom," I answer. "Is something wrong?"

"No, I'm just tired, that's all," Mom answers.

"I'll help you, Mom. I can do the vacuuming and dusting and I can fold the clothes, too," I tell her.

"Well, I could use a little help, but if you have homework, that comes first. I am looking forward to an excellent parent conference this month, Phoebe," my mom says.

"Just a tiny bit of homework, Mom. Don't worry about the parent conference. Mr. Blister loves me," I say.

That night at bedtime, when Mom tucks me into bed, she thanks me for all the cleaning I did for her. "You are such a kind little girl, Phoebe."

"Thanks, Mom. Do you think it would be

okay if Gloria came over on Saturday?" I ask her.

"Phoebe, that's five days from now," Mom says, "but, I guess so. You did help me a lot today and Gloria seems like such a nice girl."

The next day in school, I can't wait to tell Gloria the good news. She seems very happy and asks me if Amanda will be home. I think she wants it to be just the two of us.

Mr. Blister seems very unhappy with me because I never had enough time to do my homework last night. I told him I had to help my mom because she wasn't feeling well. He said this time he'd let it go, but the next time he would need a note from home explaining why I couldn't finish my homework. He also said I'd have to do last night's and tonight's homework and hand it in tomorrow.

On the way home from school, I hop on the school bus, push in and sit next to Robbie. "Hey, Robbie, wanna play this afternoon and do some homework together?" I ask. "We haven't played together in a long time."

"Yes, I'll help you with your homework, Phoebe, but you'd better come over to my house because I don't want your mother to get

mad at me if she finds out," Robbie says.

"You're the best fr—," I start to say. Then I do say, "You're the smartest, Robbie!"

Robbie and I sit on his picnic table. He does my math. I just have to write down the problems and the answers. I should think about writing my essay, but I'd rather think about having fun with Gloria.

"I don't get you, Phoebe," Robbie says. "You don't make any sense. You can add up in your head the prices of all the candy and junk we buy at the store. Then, when we put stuff back, you subtract that and you still know exactly how much it all costs. You argue with the checkout man and you are always right. You come up with the best ideas for your essays, but you never write them. You know how to fix my bike better than my dad does, and you easily figure out how to get into the garage if it's locked. So why are you always getting in trouble with Mr. Blister?"

"I don't get me either, Robbie," I sigh.

4
Cursive
Catsup

The next day in school, Mr. Blister is thrilled that I have all my math homework done. He even says, "Good job, Phoebe!" and pats me on the head like I pat Buddy Dog. But then, the worst happens! Mr. Blister tells us to take out our pencils for a spelling test.

After the test, Mr. Blister calls me up to his desk. "Phoebe, I know you didn't study these words. In fact I don't think you even looked at them. I'm going to send a note home to your mother telling her that you have to be more responsible with your homework. I want it signed and back by tomorrow. Do you understand?"

"Please, please, no, Mr. Blister! My mom will be so mad at me," I cry.

"Phoebe, your mother and I care about you," Mr. Blister says as he picks up his pen and starts to write.

Mom *is* mad! She says there is no way Gloria can come over on Saturday and that I'd be lucky if I ever had a friend over the rest of my life. I tell her it's just stupid old spelling and that's what dictionaries are for, but she doesn't care. Saturday there is no TV, no phone and no Gloria.

On Monday, when I get to school, I run through the halls to my classroom and find Gloria. "Hi, best friend in the whole world. Sorry that you couldn't come over Saturday. My mom overreacted about my homework. She's fine now." I smile at Gloria. Gloria smiles back.

"It's time to take attendance. Take your seats, please." Mr. Blister claps his hands. "I also have an announcement to make. We have a very good friend in this classroom. I was told that Gloria Von Kloppenstein took our new girl, Jooling, to the movies on Saturday. Is this correct, Gloria?"

"That's right, Mr. Blister, and we had a great time," Gloria answers.

My stomach feels sick. I can't concentrate the rest of the morning. I pray that Mr. Blister doesn't call on me. At lunch, I run up and grab Gloria's hand. "What do you have for lunch today? I've got pudding. Wanna share it with me?" I ask.

"Sure," Gloria answers, "but Jooling will have to sit with us too."

When we get to the cafeteria, Gloria sits next to Jooling and I have to squeeze in between two boys on the other side of the table. "Hey, Jooling, what's the difference between an orange and a baby?" Gloria asks, and then answers, "Nothing is the matta baby." Gloria laughs so hard and long the whole cafeteria is staring at her. Jooling grins.

That's not funny, I think to myself. She didn't even say the joke right. Gloria is not

funny. I'm funny. I'll show them both that I am funny.

"Gloria and Jooling, do you like seafood?" I take a mouthful of crackers and start to chew them until they are soggy and wet. Then I open up my mouth. "See food!" I start to laugh and choke at the same time. Sarge, the cafeteria lady, runs over. "Phoebe Flower, what are you doing?" Sarge asks.

"Oh nothing," I cough back to her. "Something just went down the wrong pipe."

"Behave yourself, Phoebe, or I'll have to write you up," Sarge tells me.

"That was gross!" Gloria says.

Jooling stares at me.

"Pass me the ketchup, please, Gloria. I need to use it for a minute," I say.

"What for?" Gloria asks. "You're through eating."

"Mr. Blister says you should practice using cursive handwriting every chance you get. I am just doing what I'm told, Gloria." I take the ketchup bottle, turn it upside down and neatly write my name on the table.

"Jooling," I say and point, "that says 'Phoebe'. That's me!"

"Phoebe Flower! Wipe up that mess right

now. Then take this note to Mr. Blister. You will have no outside play. What's the matter with you?" Sarge blasts this so loud it echoes through the cafeteria. The two boys sitting next to me howl with laughter. Gloria and Jooling stand up and take each other's hands and walk out of the cafeteria together.

So maybe writing my name wasn't so funny, I think to myself as I sit in the time-out chair in my classroom. Mr. Blister is very angry, even though I explain that I was only trying to be a good friend to Jooling. I hate sitting in time-out. There's nothing to do but stare at the walls. I'm supposed to be thinking about what I did wrong, but if I didn't do anything wrong, how could I be thinking about it? There is some cool, shiny paper in front of me. I wonder if I could make a paper airplane out of it. If I toss it just a little, everyone would think that was funny, wouldn't they? I grab the paper and quietly make a beauty of an airplane. I toss it gently through the air. It sails down on Isaiah's desk.

"Wow, this is great!" Isaiah screams. "Who made this?"

"Phoebe," Mr. Blister says, "if you can't sit

in time-out quietly for fifteen minutes, I am going to make you write one hundred times, 'I will never write with ketchup again'. Would you want to do that, Phoebe?"

"No, thank you, Mr. Blister. Then I would get a blister on my hand and then I would be Mrs. Blister," I answer, knowing for sure, that was funny.

For just about two seconds, before Mr. Blister throws his hands up in the air and screams, "THAT'S IT, PHOEBE!", I hear the class roar with laughter. I can still hear some giggles as I walk toward the office with a note in my hand for Dr. Nicely, the principal.

5

Just the Way
You Are

I push open the door to the office and smile when I see Mrs. Walkerspeaking, even though I don't feel like smiling. Mrs. Walkerspeaking is the school secretary and we're good friends. She likes me.

"Hi, Phoebe, long time no see!" Mrs. Walkerspeaking waves to me as she gets up from behind her desk and comes over to give me a hug. "What have you been doing with yourself?"

"Hi, Mrs. Walkerspeaking," I answer back. "I have to see Dr. Nicely. I think she's really going to be mad at me today."

"Oh, don't worry, Phoebe, she will be very nicely to you," Mrs. Walkerspeaking says as she laughs out loud. "Did you get that joke, Phoebe? She'll be very nicely to you."

"I do get it, Mrs. Walkerspeaking! I get it because it's funny," I tell her. "As a matter of fact, that's why I'm here. You see, I told Mr. Blister that if I had to write one hundred times that I would never write my name in ketchup again, I would get a blister and then I would be Mrs. Blister and he didn't even smile."

Mrs. Walker grins, covers her mouth, and coughs.

"See, that was funny. You make a joke about Dr. Nicely's name and we laugh. I make a joke about blisters and Mr. Blister sends me here. He just doesn't have any sense of humor. That's what the problem is. Thank you, Mrs. Walkerspeaking. I knew you would understand."

"But, Phoebe, the ketchup, part . . ." Mrs. Walkerspeaking starts to say.

Dr. Nicely's door opens and I walk right in. I've been there so many times I know exactly what to do. "Hi, Dr. Nicely!" I say and hand her Mr. Blister's note.

"What's the matter, Phoebe?" Dr. Nicely asks as she reads the note.

"Well, there is nothing the matter with me, Dr. Nicely." I start to explain. "Mrs. Walkerspeaking and I just figured out that the matter is Mr. Blister. He has no sense of humor. That is the matter. How can a teacher have no sense of humor? If I were his principal, I would tell him he has to get one before he can teach another day. I know Mrs. Walkerspeaking would agree with me, too."

"Phoebe, this note says you wrote your name in ketchup, threw a paper airplane across the classroom and then made fun of his name. Is that correct?" Dr. Nicely asks me.

"Well, it didn't actually happen like that. But, I guess, yes," I sigh.

"Phoebe, this is really getting out of hand," Dr. Nicely says in a not too nicely voice. "I am going to call your mother and see if both of your parents can come in for a conference. You've been having trouble in school for a while now and we need to find out why. Wait outside my office with Mrs. Walker and I will try to call your mother. If I can't get her on the phone, I'll need to send her a note."

I really didn't think it was a good time to tell Dr. Nicely that her name was Mrs. Walkerspeaking.

"My mother's going to be very mad," I say.

I step outside the office and my eyes start blinking fast. I don't want to cry. Mrs. Walkerspeaking gets up from behind her desk and comes over and hugs me again. "I'm so sorry, Phoebe. May I ask you, though, why did you write your name in ketchup?" "Well, Mrs. Walkerspeaking," I start to explain, "did you ever have a best friend who was pretty and smart and wore cool clothes, but—she was not funny? Well, I'm not pretty or smart and I don't wear cool clothes, but I am funny. Gloria, my best friend, wanted to be funny so that the new girl, Jooling, would like her. Gloria isn't funny at all, but Jooling laughed. I had to show Jooling what funny really was so she would stop liking Gloria and then Gloria would like me again," I say, feeling sad.

"Phoebe Flower, you are pretty and you are smart. When you grow up I bet you will be a movie star and I'll come to all your movies

36

and say to my friends, 'I knew Phoebe Flower when she was in third grade.' " Mrs. Walkerspeaking hugs me again. "When you get back to your classroom, be the best Phoebe you can be. Stop trying to be like Gloria and stop trying to make people like you. Your real friends will like you just the way you are."

"Thanks, Mrs. Walkerspeaking, but I don't have any real friends," I tell her.

"Look closer, Phoebe," Mrs. Walkerspeaking smiles at me.

The door opens and Dr. Nicely comes out to tell me she has reached my mother on the phone and that I can go back to my classroom. I wave at Mrs. Walkerspeaking and she winks at me.

6
Math
My Way

"You're just in time, Phoebe," Mr. Blister shouts as I walk into the classroom. "We are about to play a game called math challenge!"

A game is fun. Math is not. "How can we have fun with something that is unfun," I think to myself.

"Okay, is everybody ready?" Mr. Blister shouts. "I need two team captains. They will choose the teams. I will pick a boy and a girl captain, but I want each of them to pick boys and girls. The winning team will get free ice cream for lunch on Friday, so please try hard. The boy captain will be Robbie Vaughn III and the girl captain will be Gloria Von Kloppenstein. Gloria, you may pick first."

I sit up straight, look right at Gloria and smile like a best friend should.

"Jooling!" Gloria calls. She doesn't even look at me.

"Phoebe!" Robbie yells and grins a big disgusting grin.

"What?" I say.

"Phoebe, Robbie just picked you first to be on his team. Go stand next to him and, please, no more trouble from you today," Mr. Blister sighs.

I have had bad days, but this has been the worst day I've had since I was born. Robbie and Gloria continue to pick their teams until every one in the class is standing.

Gloria only has two boys on her team and Robbie only has two girls. I don't want to be on Robbie's team. I know Gloria picked Jooling because she is smart, but that shouldn't matter. I have decided that Gloria is not very good at being a best friend.

"Okay, the first question is for Robbie since Gloria picked first. Robbie," Mr. Blister begins, "five pieces of coal, one carrot and one scarf are lying on the lawn. Nobody put them on the lawn, so what is the reason that they are there? You have thirty seconds to think of the answer."

"I know the answer," Robbie says after twenty seconds pass. "A snowman melted. I couldn't think of the answer right away because when Phoebe and I make snowmen we don't use coal. We use colored markers and push them in so they won't fall out. Then the snowman has colored eyes and colored buttons."

"Great job, Robbie. Now your turn, Gloria," Mr. Blister continues. "What is twice the half of two? You also have thirty seconds."

"Easy, Mr. Blister. The answer is two and one half," Gloria answers.

"Sorry, Gloria. The answer is two. These are tricky questions, aren't they?" Mr. Blister smiles.

Gloria stomps to her desk and sits down with a pout on her face.

"Okay, Phoebe, it's your turn. If two

peacocks lay two eggs in two days how many eggs can one peacock lay in four days? You have thirty seconds."

"I don't need thirty seconds, Mr. Blister. The answer is zero. Peacocks don't lay eggs," I answer.

"Very good, Phoebe." Mr. Blister looks surprised. "Jooling, your turn. Listen carefully."

The math challenge continues until only two kids are left standing. One is Jooling and one is me. It's my turn.

"Phoebe, this is a tricky question. Are you ready?" Mr. Blister asks me.

"Fire away, Mr. Blister," I answer, wondering when I got so smart.

"A farmer had four haystacks in one field and two times as many in each of his other two fields. He put the haystacks from all three fields together. How many haystacks did he now have?" asks Mr. Blister

I think about the trip to the farm we took in first grade and answer, "Only one, Mr. Blister, one big one."

"Wow, Phoebe, you sure are good at these tricky questions," says Mr. Blister.

"Why do you think I picked her first?" Robbie yells from his seat. "I love ice cream!"

"Okay, if Jooling gets this right, then we'll have two more questions." Mr. Blister explains. "If, she gets it wrong, Robbie's team is the winning team. Ready, Jooling?"

Jooling nods her head.

"Jooling, how many two cent stamps are in a dozen?" Mr. Blister asks.

That's so easy, I think to myself. He gives her such baby questions. A dozen anything is a dozen. The answer is twelve.

"Six, Mr. Blister," Jooling answers.

I want to jump up and touch the ceiling and scream, but for the first time since I've been in third grade, I control myself, stand still and look sad for Jooling. I even say, "Ahh, that's too bad."

Robbie's team is shouting, "Yea, Phoebe!" I feel so smart.

"That was a tricky question, boys and girls," Mr. Blister says, "Let's not make Jooling feel bad."

"Congratulations, Phoebe," Gloria says to me on the way to the bus. "I'm sorry I didn't pick you first, but I knew you'd understand and I didn't think Jooling would. Are we still best friends?"

"Sure, Gloria. I understand," I tell her. I really don't.

I can't wait to get home and tell my mom about the math challenge. She won't believe how smart I am. When I burst through the door, my mom is standing in the living room with her arms folded in front of her.

"Mom, I had the greatest day! Wait until you hear!" I scream at her.

Quietly, almost too quietly, my mom says, "A great day? A great day? Is that what you had? So, having a great day means writing your name with ketchup on the table, making fun of your teacher and being sent to the principal's office? PHOEBE FLOWER, that is not a great day to me . . ."

"But, Mom," I start to talk.

". . . and Dr. Nicely wants your father and me to meet with her in her office next week to discuss what we should do about your behavior. Go to your room, Phoebe, and get your homework done right now. I am so angry I can't even see straight."

I run upstairs and jump into bed and pull the covers over my head.

7
Add, Subtract, or What?

For the next week, I try to be a perfect kid in Mr. Blister's third grade classroom. I get almost all my homework done. I raise my hand if I need to talk or sharpen my pencil. I only go to the bathroom twice in the morning and three times in the afternoon. Mr. Blister asks me if I'm feeling okay. I am thinking that if I do everything right, my dad and mom will have to cancel the meeting with Dr. Nicely.

Then, on Saturday, I hear my mom telling Amanda to clean her room because Dad is driving in on Sunday and he'll be sleeping in her room. I can't believe he's still coming! I've been so good at school all this week.

"Why's Dad coming?" Amanda asks.

"He and I have to go to a meeting at school," Mom answers.

I feel sick to my stomach. What do principals tell parents to do with kids that write with ketchup on the table? What if they send me to a jail and make me eat ketchup sandwiches every day for the rest of my life?

"So, Dad, when are you heading back?" I ask my dad as he tucks me into bed Sunday night.

"When we get this whole mess settled, Phoebe," Dad answers.

"Oh yeah, that," I answer, pretending the whole mess is about the broken swing set in the back yard.

Monday morning my mom and dad ask me to sit down on the living room couch because they want to talk to me. They tell me there is a meeting in Dr. Nicely's office at nine o'clock and "we" all have to be there. Mom told me that I will be riding to school with them. I start to ask who the "we" are, but then I have a picture in my mind of Mr. Blister running into Dr. Nicely's office and telling all of them that I have become the perfect student and they can all go home and forget about the ketchup. I like having that picture.

When Mom and Dad and I walk into the office, Mrs. Walkerspeaking stands up and shakes their hands. "I just love, Phoebe," she tells them. "If I could pick anyone in this school to come and be my daughter, I would pick your Phoebe."

"Thank you," my dad says, "apparently everyone at this school doesn't feel the same, Mrs. Walkerspeaking. Is that really your name?"

"No, but that's what Phoebe calls me, so it's fine with me," Mrs. Walkerspeaking says. "By the way, did Phoebe ever tell you about the time I lost my good diamond earring down the heater vent?"

"I'm not sure if she did." My dad looks at my mom.

"Well," Mrs. Walkerspeaking continues, not

waiting for an answer, "I called down to Phoebe's room and asked Mr. Blister to please send Phoebe down to the office and help me figure out a way to get it out. Phoebe borrowed yarn from the art teacher and attached a safety pin and dropped the yarn and pin down the heater vent and fished the earring out in no time flat. I just knew she could do it! She is one clever little girl."

I smile at Mrs. Walkerspeaking.

"Thanks, but is Dr. Nicely ready to see us yet?" Dad says without one tiny little smile.

"Yes, sir, Mr. Flower. You may enter her office now." Mrs. Walkerspeaking opens Dr. Nicely's office door.

Mr. Blister and Dr. Nicely are sitting at a round table with five chairs. I am so nervous I feel like I am going to wet my pants. I don't think Mr. Blister is going to tell everyone to forget the ketchup story.

"Please sit down," Dr. Nicely says with a big smile. "How are you today, Phoebe?"

"Fine," I answer. How does she think I am? I want to charge down the hall and out the front door and run until I'm in the next year.

"Phoebe, I want to talk to your parents about your behavior in school. I want you to know what we are discussing, so that it is not a secret. Mr. Blister and I are going to talk about the problems you are having. We want things to go better for you in school. Do you understand?"

I nod my head.

"You can go to your classroom now, but I want you to know what's going on here, okay?" Dr. Nicely tells me.

I nod my head again as I get up and open the door and walk as fast as I can out of the office.

I wait one whole day and nobody says one word about that meeting.

The night before Dad leaves to go back to New York, he knocks on my door.

"Enter at your own risk," I say.

"It's me, Phoebe. I just came to tell you I'm leaving for New York tomorrow. You know, Phoebe," my dad begins, "I just want to tell you one thing. You have to work hard if you ever want to make something out of your life."

"I know Dad, and I'm really trying," I tell him.

"Try harder, Phoebe." Dad hugs me. "I love you and I know you can do it."

After Dad leaves, Amanda decides to pay me a visit in my bedroom. This must be my lucky day.

"I know what's wrong with you!" she whispers, "I heard Mom and Dad talking in the kitchen just now. Dr. Nicely told Mom and Dad that she and Mr. Blister think you might have 'add'. They spelled it out 'A-D-D' because they thought you might be listening and they didn't think you would understand if they spelled it."

"You shouldn't have been listening, Amanda," I say, wishing I had been listening too.

"Okay, then I won't tell you what else they said. I won't tell you about how you have to go see Dr. Getset, and how you might have to take medicine and Mr. Blister is going to write notes to Mom about how you act every single day," Amanda smiles.

"Well, if I have 'add', then you must have 'subtract'. So just subtract yourself from my room, Amanda, right now. You are making me want to cry," I yell.

Maybe I do have "add", I thought. I did win the math challenge for Robbie's team.

Maybe "add" is a disease that kids who do

great in math challenges have. Maybe it's a good thing to have. Maybe Amanda doesn't know everything . . . maybe she does.

8
Mom's Secret Confession

The next day, I get to the bus stop early so I can talk to Robbie.

"Robbie, wanna hear something awful?" I ask him.

"No," he says.

"Well, it isn't awful for you, but it is for me, so do ya wanna?" I ask again.

"I guess," Robbie says.

"Well, my parents had to go meet with Dr. Nicely on Monday to find out why I'm always getting in trouble and Amanda said she heard them talking and that I have an 'add' disease and I have to go to a doctor and take medicine and get notes home every day. Do you think it's because I won the math challenge?"

"Phoebe, why don't you ask your mother? She'll tell you," Robbie says.

"I guess I can, Robbie, but I'm sort of scared," I say.

That night at bedtime, I hug my mom so tight I think she almost stops breathing.

"I love you too, Phoebe. Are you okay?" she asks.

"I'm fine, Mom," I answer. "Do you think Gloria can come over this weekend?"

"I thought you and Gloria weren't getting along," Mom says.

"Well, we weren't, but I think it's because I can never have her over. She just forgets that we're best friends," I tell her.

"Did you get all your homework done?" Mom asks me.

"I added all my math if that's what you mean," I tell her.

"Well, not really, but that's good. Do you need any help with your homework?" Mom wants to know.

"No, I'm pretty good at add . . . ing," I say.

"Why are you acting so weird and saying 'adding' so slowly, like your tongue is getting stuck on your teeth? Did you bite it tonight at dinner?" Mom asks me.

"Because Amanda said I have the 'add' disease," I blurted out, "and that's why Dad came here and now I have to go see Dr. Getset and take medicine and get notes home every minute and I want to know what's wrong with me and why aren't you telling me."

"Phoebe, honey, let's have a nice talk," Mom says as she hops onto my bed and puts her arms around me. "I am so sorry I didn't say anything sooner. I know I should have, but your father said he would take care of everything and talk to you about trying harder. That's why I didn't say anything to you. We did talk to Dr. Nicely. We're concerned about why you are not getting your homework done, and why you have trouble sitting still and paying attention in class, and why your room and your desk are always a mess."

"But Amanda says I have 'add'. What's

that?" I ask.

"Amanda shouldn't have been listening. It's A.D.D. and that's short for a Attention Deficit Disorder. That's what Dr. Nicely thinks you may have. It means that you have trouble paying attention, but it also means that you are very clever and you sometimes think in more creative ways than most people. Sometimes you start something and then you start something else without finishing the first thing and that creates your messes. You are very smart, but you don't know how to show it in the way that school wants you to. You know how you don't like to sit and do your homework and how you daydream and how you hate to wait your turn?"

"You mean some people *like* to do home-work and be third in line?" My mouth drops open. I am shocked.

"Well, I guess they don't mind it like you do," Mom tells me.

"And I don't know what's wrong with daydreaming, Mom," I say. Yesterday, Mr. Blister told me to stop daydreaming, and I told him I had just remembered that it was Buddy Dog's birthday and I had to go get him an extra treat after school. I bet no one else in

the family remembered it was Buddy Dog's birthday."

"Exactly!" Mom answers.

"So, do I have to take medicine and see Dr. Getset and get notes home everyday from Mr. Blister?" I wonder out loud.

"We don't know," Mom says. "All we want is for you to be happy and do well in school and know we love you. Dr. Getset just wants to talk to you and do some testing."

"Phoebe, I have a little secret to tell you, too," my mom snuggles closer to me. "When I was a little girl, I had problems in school too. I think I might have mentioned this before. I would stare out the window and watch the clouds and make up stories in my head about the sky monsters. I was quiet and didn't call out like you do, but I had a lot of trouble finishing my schoolwork." "I do understand what you're going through, Phoebe."

"Did you have to go see a doctor and get notes home and take medicine?" I ask my mom.

"No, because, back then, there was no one to help me, Phoebe. My teachers just got upset with me and ignored me. I think they thought I was just lazy. I wanted to be a doctor when I grew up, but I didn't go to college because it was so hard for me to study. I had to read things over and over again because I would daydream and forget what I was reading. You are so lucky. People at your school want to help you." Mom hugged me tight.

"Do you think I'll ever do better in school, Mom?" I ask and yawn.

"Yes, Phoebe, I think that with everyone working together, trying to understand how you think, and figuring out how you can get your work done, things *will* get better. Now get some sleep. Remember, I love you, Phoebe, and we are all trying to help you."

"Good night. I love you, too, Mom."

"Sleep tight," Mom tells me.

9

A Very
High Five!!!

About a week after my mom and I have our talk about ADD, Mr. Blister calls me over to the classroom door and says, "Phoebe, I want you to meet Dr. Getset."

Dr. Getset is bald with a white beard and mustache. I've seen him in school before, but I pretend I don't know who he is. "How do you do?" I ask. I heard someone say that once, on TV.

"I'm fine, Phoebe, and how do you do?" Dr. Getset asks me. I can tell he wants me to like him. I don't think I will.

"Come on down to my office, Phoebe. We can play some games." Dr. Getset turns and walks down the hall. Mr. Blister nods for me to follow him.

When we get to his office, Dr. Getset smiles and says, "Do you have any questions for me, Phoebe?"

"Yeah," I say, "is that really your name?"

"Sure is, Dr. Mark Getset, that's me!" he says. "I even have a dog named 'Go'. When I walk down the street with my dog, the neighbors yell, 'Hey, Mark Getset and Go.' Get it, Phoebe?" Dr. Getset laughs.

I guess that was pretty funny. Maybe I will like him. I wonder if I should tell him my Mr. Blister joke.

Dr. Getset is a pretty nice guy. He asks me questions and listens carefully to my answers. He asks, "Phoebe, what's your favorite thing to do?"

"Daydream, Dr. Getset," I answer.

He says, "I love to do that too, Phoebe, especially when I'm working in my garden."

We play games and he asks me questions and I have to do math problems in my head. He shows me pictures and I have to tell him what I see. When it's time for me to go I ask, "Dr. Getset, is there something wrong with me?"

"Not at all, Phoebe, you are a very smart little girl." Dr. Getset puts his hand on my shoulder. "You just do things a little differently, and some things, like paying attention and getting your work done, are harder for you. I have helped lots of other kids with these problems do better in school. What do you think about that?" "I don't know," I answer, "but it sounds good to me."

Once a week, I go to Dr. Getset's room. Today, when I see him I am feeling pretty sad and I don't know why.

"What's the matter, Phoebe?" Dr. Getset asks me.

"I don't know," I tell him. "I just hate coming to school."

"Phoebe, do you know why you are coming to see me?" Dr. Getset asks.

"Well, sort of," I answer. "Mom says I'm clever and smart, but I don't feel clever or smart.

I am always getting into trouble with Mr. Blister."

"Let me try to explain, Phoebe," Dr. Getset says. "Do you remember how you rescued Jack and how you helped Mrs. Walker find her earring and how you won the math challenge?"

"Yeah, of course I do," I tell him.

"Well, Phoebe, you were a heroine because you think in a different way than most kids, but that's why you get into trouble, too," Dr. Getset continues. "You like life to be exciting. It's hard for you to read textbooks and study spelling words and practice multiplication because your mind wanders to things that are more interesting to you. Then, when you have a choice of doing your school work or thinking of fun exciting things, you choose the fun things and that's how you get into trouble. Does that make sense to you, Phoebe?"

"Yes, I guess so," I tell him.

"Dr. Nicely and Mr. Blister want to help you. It's important that you do well in school and it's also important that you understand how you think," Dr. Getset says. "I am the lucky man who is here to help you. So, Phoebe, on your mark, get set . . . let's go."

64

When I get back to the classroom, Mr. Blister tells me that the class just went outside to the playground. I hurry out to tell Robbie that Dr. Getset is going to help me. Robbie is running straight at me. He looks like he is about to cry.

"Phoebe, you've gotta help me. Please!" Robbie yells. "Isaiah made a paper airplane out of my essay. He tossed it and it landed in that tree over there. Will you climb up and get it for me, please?"

I am trying so hard to stay out of trouble. If I get caught in that tree, I'll be in big trouble again. I know Robbie is afraid of heights, but it does serve him right. The essay isn't due for two more days. He always has his work done ahead of time. Robbie would do anything for me, though.

"Okay," I say slowly.

"Hurry, Phoebe," Robbie calls as I head toward the tree, "the bell is going to ring in about ten minutes."

I pull myself up on the lowest branch of the tree. I can see Robbie's paper about six branches up. This is so easy. I don't know what Robbie's afraid of.

"Hey, Robbie," I hear a group of boys call,

"come on and play football with us."

Robbie looks up at me and shrugs his shoulders and runs off to play with his friends. I reach the spot where his essay has landed and grab it off the branch. No wonder the paper airplane went up in the tree. Isaiah didn't make it right. I'll have to show him how to make it so it flies straight. I start to climb down the tree.

"Come on, let's sit under this tree, Elizabeth," I hear Gloria say. I look down and see Gloria, Elizabeth and three other girls from my class walking toward my tree. I stop moving and hold my breath. They put their sweaters on the grass and sit right underneath me. "Please, oh, please, don't look up," I think to myself.

"I don't know why you're such good friends with Jooling, Gloria," Elizabeth says.

"I think she can speak better English than she does. I bet she just likes the attention she gets."

The other three girls nodded their heads.

"What do you think, Gloria?" Elizabeth asks.

"She's okay," Gloria answers.

"Oh, sure she's okay, but she acts like she's

so pretty and all the boys think so too," says Elizabeth. "I don't think she's very pretty at all, do you?"

"She's not bad," answers Gloria.

"Not bad, maybe, but I wouldn't be caught dead in the clothes she wears. Would you?" Elizabeth asks.

"I guess I wouldn't," Gloria laughs. "Her skirt is pretty ugly."

The bell rings and all five girls get up giggling and head toward the school.

"Wow," I think to myself, "I guess Gloria doesn't really like Jooling after all. She must have just wanted Mr. Blister to think she liked her. That is great news for me. Gloria and I can still be best friends." I hop out of the tree and skip all the way into school.

Tonight, I sit at my desk thinking it's the first time in my whole life that I'm excited to start my homework. I start to write the title of my essay, "I Am Most Thankful For My Best Friend." That doesn't sound good. I rip it up. "The Friend I Am Most Thankful For." "I Am Thankful For Gloria." No, it just doesn't seem right. I throw seven papers in the basket and stare at my desk.

I hear a knock on the door. "Come in," I say.

"Phoebe, can I help you?" Mom asks as she rubs my back.

"I need all the help I can get." "I just can't write it, Mom," I tell her. "It doesn't sound right."

"You might be thinking too hard. Writing about your best friend should be easy. Just write down what your heart says to you, Phoebe." Mom hugs me. "Call me if you need my help."

All of a sudden, I don't need help. I write my essay and then I sleep all night.

The next day at school, I wait until it's my turn to read my essay.

Finally, Mr. Blister asks, "Phoebe Flower, it's your turn to read. Did you do your homework?"

"Sure did, Mr. Blister," I tell him.

I walk to the front of the room and clear my throat. "I Am Most Thankful For My Best Friend," I begin.

Gloria turns, smiles and looks around the room. "We all know who that is," she whispers loudly.

68

"My best friend knows when I'm happy and when I'm sad. My best friend knows when I need to be alone and when I need a friend. My best friend helps me and I help my best friend, too, even when I don't want to. My best friend says nice things to me and thinks I'm smart. I don't have to pretend to be somebody else when I'm with my best friend. I can be me, and do things differently, and know that's okay." I look up and breathe. "Mrs. Walkerspeaking said, 'Look closer, Phoebe, and you'll find your real friends.' I didn't know Mrs. Walkerspeaking meant look next door."

Gloria's mouth drops open and her smile disappears.

"Robert Vaughn III is always first when I need a friend. I am most thankful for Robbie." I take a deep breath.

The classroom is as quiet as falling snowflakes. Not one kid speaks. Mr. Blister clears his throat, but doesn't say a word.

I shove my essay into my pocket and walk back to my seat. I have to walk by Robbie's desk. He stares at me and stands up. I stare back at him. I hope I didn't embarrass Robbie and he'll never like me again.

"Stop!" Robbie says. He puts his hand up.

"High five, Phoebe!" Robbie smiles.
"High five, Robbie!" I smile back.